1 MONTH OF
FREE
READING

at
www.ForgottenBooks.com

By purchasing this book you are eligible for one month membership to ForgottenBooks.com, giving you unlimited access to our entire collection of over 1,000,000 titles via our web site and mobile apps.

To claim your free month visit:
www.forgottenbooks.com/free192040

ISBN 978-1-5284-6336-2
PIBN 10192040

This book is a reproduction of an important historical work. Forgotten Books uses
state-of-the-art technology to digitally reconstruct the work, preserving the original format
whilst repairing imperfections present in the aged copy. In rare cases, an imperfection in
the original, such as a blemish or missing page, may be replicated in our edition. We do,
however, repair the vast majority of imperfections successfully; any imperfections that
remain are intentionally left to preserve the state of such historical works.

THOMAS W. JACKSON.

On a Slow Train Through Arkansaw

By THOS. W. JACKSON

FUNNY RAILROAD STORIES—SAYINGS OF THE
SOUTHERN DARKIES—ALL THE LATEST
AND .BEST MINSTREL JOKES
OF THE DAY

THIS BOOK SENT POST PAID TO ANY
ADDRESS ON RECEIPT OF 25 CENTS

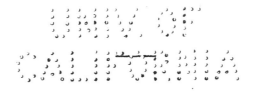

THOS. W. JACKSON, Publisher
CHICAGO, ILL.

On a Slow Train Through Arkansaw

———

You are not the only pebble on the beach for there is a little rock in Arkansaw. It was down in the state of Arkansaw I rode on the slowest train I ever saw. It stopped at every house. When it come to a double house it stopped twice. They made so many stops I said, "Conductor, what have we stopped for now?" He said, "There are some cattle on the track." We ran a little ways further and stopped again. I said, "What is the matter now?" He said, "We have caught up with those cattle again." We made pretty good time for about two miles. One old cow got her tail caught in the cow-catcher and she ran off down the track with the train. The cattle bothered us so much they had to take the cow-catcher off the engine and put it on the hind end of the train to keep the cattle from jumping up in the sleeper. A lady said, "Conductor, can't this train make any better time than this?" He said, "If you ain't satisfied with this train, you can get off and walk." She said she would, only her folks didn't expect her till the train got there. A lady handed the conductor two tickets, one whole ticket and a half ticket. He said,

5

"Who is the half ticket for?" She said, "My boy." The conductor said, "He's not a boy;

THE SLOW TRAIN

he's a man. Under twelve, half fare, over twelve, full fare." She said, "He was under twelve when we started."

The news agent came through. He was an old man with long gray whiskers. I said, "Old

ON THE SLOW TRAIN

man, I thought they always had boys on the train to sell the pop corn, chewing gum and candy." He said he was a boy when he started. They stopped so often one of the passengers tried to commit suicide. He ran ahead for half a mile, laid down on the track, but he starved to death before the train got there.

We had a narrow escape of being killed. Just as we got on the middle of a high bridge the engineer discovered it was on fire, but we went right across. Just as the last car got over, the bridge fell. I said, "Conductor, how did we ever get across without going down?" He said, "Some train robbers held us up."

We ran a little further and stopped again. Some one asked the conductor what was wrong. He said a cow had kicked the fireman in the jaw. The engineer had stopped to tie the cow's foot up.

The conductor collected half fare from a lady for her little girl. It made her so mad she asked the conductor what that said on his cap. He said, "Train conductor." She said it ought to be "Train robber." He said he only took what was fare.

There was a lady on the train with a baby. When the conductor asked her for her ticket, she said she didn't have any, the baby had swallowed it. The conductor punched the baby.

There were three kinds of passengers who rode on that train. First class, Second class and Third class. I said, "Conductor, what is the difference between the First class and Third class passengers, they are all riding in the same car?" He said, "Just wait a while and I will show you." We ran a little ways and stopped again. The conductor came in and said, "First class passengers, keep your seats; Second class passengers, get off and walk; Third class passengers, get off and push."

For a crooked road, she was the limit. In order to get the engine around the curves they had a hinge in the boiler. The fireman had a wooden leg and was crossed-eyed, half of the time he was shoveling coal in the headlight instead of the fire-box. It was so crooked we met ourself coming back. The curves were so short they called them corners. The engineer had to shave every day to keep the rocks from knocking off his whiskers.

The conductor was the tallest man I ever saw. I said, "Conductor, what makes you so tall?" He said it was because he had had his leg pulled so often. He said he was born in the top of a ten story building. He came high, but they had to have him.

He said he had been running on that road for thirty years, and had only taken in one fare, that was the World's Fair.

An old lady said to the porter, "Are you the colored porter?" He said, no, he wasn't colored he was born that way. She said, "I gave you a dollar, where is my change?" He said, "This car goes through; there is no change."

There was a Dutchman on the train, he was trying to ride on a meal ticket. The conductor told him he would have to pay his fare. He said, "How much does it cost to ride to the next station?" The conductor said, "Thirty cents." The Dutchman said, "I will give you twenty-five." The conductor told him it would cost him thirty. The Dutchman said, "Before I will give more than twenty-five I will walk." The conductor stopped the train and put him off. The Dutchman ran ahead of the engine and started to walk. The engineer began to blow the whistle. The

Dutchman said, "You can vissel all you vant, I wont come back."

There was an old man and woman on the train by the name of Jessup.   There happened to be a place where the train stopped by the name of Jessup's Cut.   The old man went to the car ahead. When the brakeman came in and hollered, "Jessup's Cut!" the old woman jumped up and hollered, "My God! who cut Jessup?"

They ran a little ways further and stopped again. Somebody said, "Conductor, what have we stopped for now?"   He said, "We have reached the top of the hill.   It is now down grade; we will make a little better time and have an entire change of scenery."   And so we did.

"Are you married?"
"Yes, I married a spiritualist."
"How are you getting along?"
"Medium."

I hear they are going to vaccinate the entire police force of Chicago.

I don't see what they want to do that for, a policeman never catches anything.

"We had a big wooden-wedding over at our house."
"How was that?"
"My sister married a blockhead."

"Do you know that my sister is a duchess now?"
"No.   How did she come to be a duchess?"
"She married a Dutchman."

"I got a letter from father the other day. He has gone in the hog business. I wrote and told told him that there was lots of money in hogs, to stay with it."

"What do you know about hogs?"

"I know all about hogs; I was raised with them."

"You must be from Missouri."

"Do you think that Shakespeare wrote all those plays that they say he did?"

"I don't know, I never thought much about it, but when I die, if I am fortunate enough to go to Heaven, I will ask him."

"In case he ain't there, then what?"

"Oh, well! then you ask him."

"My girl is a dressmaker; she makes wrappers for cigars. There is just one thing wrong with her; she is cross-eyed. She is a good girl; she is honest but she looks crooked."

"Do you read the papers?"

"Yes."

"Have you noticed the number of railroad accidents that have happened lately? Just the other night at a wedding it so happened that Johnny Carr was going to be married to a young lady of the same name. Just as the preacher was pronouncing the ceremony a rifle ball came through the window, struck the preacher in the breast and killed him."

"Well, what has that got to do with a railroad accident?"

"They say he was killed while coupling cars.

"Only yesterday at the hotel I am stopping at,

one of the chamber-maids was found lying in a room dead; her false hair had come down, wrapped around her neck and choked her to death. They say her death was caused by a misplaced switch."

The only difference between you and a man that takes the wool off a lamb's back and dyes it is, he is a lamb's dyer and you are a d—— l——.

What is the difference between that ten dollars you owe me and Tennessee.

What is the difference?

Tennessee I will see. The ten you owe me I will never see.

There was a little town on the line called Holder. There was a newly married couple on the train. They were holding hands and warming right up to one another when the brakeman came in and hollered, "Holder! Holder!" He said it was all right if he did, they were married.

The conductor told a fellow that the next place was where he got off. He said, "Which end of the car shall I get off of?" The conductor said, "Either one; both ends stop."

There was a young fellow on the train. He couldn't get a seat. He was walking up and down the aisle and swearing. There was a preacher in the car. He said, "Young man, do you know where you are going, sir? You are going straight to Hell." He said, "I don't give a darn; I've got a round trip ticket."

The brakeman came in and hollered, "Twenty minutes for dinner!" When the train stopped we all rushed for the dining-room, I ordered two soft boiled eggs.   When the waiter brought them in, she opened one and said, "Shall I open the other?"

I said, "No, open the window."

She said, "Ain't the eggs all right?"

I said, "Yes, they are all right, but I think they have been mislaid."

One fellow in the excitement drank a cup of yeast thinking it was buttermilk.   He rose immediately.

A FOUR MILE RUN

The waiter was handing me my coffee just as the conductor was hollering, "All aboard."   She slipped and fell and spilled the coffee down my back. When she got up she said, "Excuse me, will you have some more?"

I said, "No, you can bring me an umbrella."

When I looked out I saw the train was going. It was down grade, I had to run it for four miles; caught the hind car; just as I pulled myself up on the steps the train stopped, backed in on the siding and laid four hours to take on wood.

When we started a young lady asked the conductor if her uncle would meet her at the depot when she got off. Of course he was supposed to know.

At one place we stopped a fellow ran up to the conductor and said, "Is this my train?" He said, "I don't think so. The company has got their name on it." The fellow said, "I am going to take it." The conductor said, "You want to be careful about that, for there has been several trains missed here lately."

The stations were so close together when they stopped at one they had to back up to whistle for the next.

There were some of the wealthiest ladies on that train I ever saw. The train stopped, one lady said to the other, "This is your town, and the next one is mine."

Pretty soon they hollered out, "Skeetersville!" That was my town where I got off. I saw a sign that read "Hotel." I went over and registered.

They gave me a room on the first floor, that is from the roof. It was one of those rooms when you rent it the roof uses it. When I went to bed I had a creeping sensation come over me. I got up and told the landlord that there were bugs in the bed. He said there wasn't a single bed-bug in the house! I told him that he was right about it, they were all married and had large families.

I remember the hotel was on the bluff and it was run on bluff. Skeetersville was a very appro-

HOTEL SCENE IN ARKANSAW

priate name for the place, for the musquitors was all there. They would come around and look on the register to see what room you had. The landlord told me he had just adopted a new set of rules. He handed me a list of them. They read something like this:

Rule One: In order to prevent the guests from carrying fruit from the table, there will be no fruit.

Married men without baggage will leave their wives in the office.

Old and feeble gentlemen will not be allowed to play in the halls.

Guests will not be allowed to use Indian clubs or dumbbells in their rooms. If they want exercise they can go in the kitchen and beat the steak. I set right up to the table and beat mine.

Guests will not be allowed to tip the waiters, as it is liable to cause them to break the dishes. (I promise you there was no dishes broken while I was there.)

Guests at. this hotel wishing fine board, will please call for saw dust. Biscuits found riveted together can be opened with a chisel furnished by the waiter. The use of dynamite is positively prohibited.

Guests needn't mind paying their board, as the hotel is supported by a good foundation.

Guests on retiring at night will leave their money with the night clerk, for he will get it anyhow.

If you want the bellboy, wring a towel.

If you get hungry during the night, take a roll in bed.

Base-ball players wanting exercise will find a pitcher on the table.

If you want to write take a sheet off the bed.

If you find the bed to be a little buggy and you have a nightmare, just hitch the mare to the buggy and drive off.

The landlord took me out for a drive. There is some fine farms down there. He showed me a farm that you could raise anything on. He said they could raise potatoes as large as your head. They could raise cabbage that would weigh over a hundred pounds. I said, "This is certainly a remarkable country. How do you account for it all?"

He said, "It is the climate. That is the secret of it all. It is the climate." I said, "Old man, do you know that in the City of Chicago there is a building that is twenty-two stories high that hasn't got any stairs or elevator to it?"

"How do they get up in it?"

"They climb it."

He said, "Do you know, that all we need in this country is a little more rain and a little better society." I said, "That is all that Hell needs."

I had only been there about a week when the landlord told me I had been bombarding against his house. I told him I hadn't been doing any bombarding, but I had been doing some bum boarding.

You couldn't get a square meal. They fed us on round tables.

CONUNDRUMS.

Did you ever hear the story about the black crow? No, I never did. It's a bird.

Did you ever hear the story about the two holes in the ground. No. Well, well.

What is the greatest neglected vegetable in the world. A policeman's beat.

Why is a pocket handkerchief like a ship at sea? Because it gets many a hard blow and occasionally goes around the horn.

Why are eggs always cheaper on the docks? Because the ships lay to.

Suppose you should break your knee, where should you go to get another? To Africa, that is where the negroes.

Can you tell me the difference between a pair of pants and a pie?

What is the difference?

A pair of pants has to be cut before they are made: a pie has to be made before it is cut.

Why is a horse with his head hanging down like next Monday?

Because its neck's weak.

Why does a hen lay an egg? Because it is beyond the power of Carrie Nation to hatch it.

Suppose a lady should break her knee, where should she go to get another? To Jerusalem, where the Shee-neys grow.

Why do the stars in the American Flag represent the stars in Heaven? Because it is beyond the power of any nation on earth to pull them down.

What is the difference between Christian Science and a lean woman? One is a humbug, the other is a bum hug.

If you kiss a young lady she calls it faith. If you kiss a married woman she calls it hope. If you kiss an old maid she calls it charity.

———

My next stop was Pottsville. When I got there the county fair was going on. It looked like Fourth of July. Talk about the streets of Cairo! they wasn't in it with Pottsville. I went out to the fair grounds.   I met a one-legged man selling lead pencils.   I asked him how business was. He said he couldn't kick.

I saw a fellow turning a hand-organ with a sign on his hat that said, "Help me, I am blind."   I said to him, "How do I know you are blind? You prove to me you are blind, and I will give you a quarter."   He said, "Let me see the quarter."

I went a little ways further; saw a sign that said, "Fortunes told"; went in and had mine told. The fortune teller looked at my hand and told mine.   He said I was going to get married and have lots of clothes.   I asked him how he could tell. He said by my clothes line.   He told me I had been eating onions.   How do you suppose he knew that?   I told him I hadn't breathed it to a soul except him.   He said that I would be without money until I was forty years old and then I would be used to it.

I saw a lot of fellows throwing balls at babies. You get a cigar for every baby you hit.   I throwed for ten minutes, and never hit a baby.   I began to get homesick right away.   I suppose it was because I missed the children.

I went to the postoffice.   There I saw some signs that read, "Postoffice open from now till then." "From here to there."   "Pistol cards for sale." "Leave your address with the undertaker." "Stamp your letters and not your feet."   "Lick the stamps and not the Post Master."   "Office closes at six o'clock on the last Saturday of each week."   "By order of the Post Hole office man."

A man came in and said to the Post Master, "Is there a letter here for me?"   The Post Master said, "What is the name, please?" He said, "Louder." The Post Master said, "I want to know your name." He said, "Louder. J. H. Louder. If you wasn't working for Uncle Sam I'd take a tooth pick and come around behind there and clean your ears."

I went to the hotel, picked up a paper, read the heading of a piece that said, "Big Railroad Wreck. No one hurt! Ten Texas steers and a brakeman killed!" The heading of another piece read like this, "Big shoe store burnt in the East. One thousand soles lost, all the heels were saved." I read another piece that said, "A man jumped in the river and committed suicide! They say there was a woman at the bottom of it!"

I read some of the advertisements.

One read, "Wanted, young lady to work in a bakery. She must be from the East and well bred and she will get her dough every Saturday night."

Another read, "Wanted a man and wife to work on a farm. They must speak German and French and understand horses and cows."

"Young man wants position in bank handling money. Has no objections to leaving town."

"A man that never done a day's work in his life wants a position as night watchman."

"Large dog for sale   Will eat anything. Very fond of children."

While I was there I was arrested for gambling. The judge fined me ten dollars. I said: "Judge, I wasn't playing for money, I was playing for chips." He said chips was just the same as money. So I gave him ten dollars worth of chips.

In Arkansaw they believe in doing everything

right. I stopped at a place where there was one doctor, two shoe makers and a blacksmith. The doctor killed a man. They didn't want to be without a doctor, so they hung one of the shoe makers.

I stopped at one place where they had lost all track of the day of the week. They were holding church on Monday for Sunday. Some of the people down there have a queer way of naming their children. I stopped with a family that had two twin boys. One was named Pete and the other Repete. At another place they had two twin girls. One they called Kate, the other Duplicate. I stopped with a family by the name of Wind. They had a daughter. Her name was Helen Augusta Wind.

We came to a sign in the forks of a road that read like this, "Take the right hand road for the distillery. If you can't read, ask the blacksmith." At another place I was at they were going to have an entertainment. It was to be home talent, of course. I received an invitation and was also asked to take part in the play, which I agreed to do. They put my name on the program, and, of course, I was expected to do something. I remember the first number on the program was a young lady. She came out to sing. She had a kind of a Montana voice. It was a beaut. It was Hell-ena. She had it vaccinated but it didn't take.

The next was a young fellow. He sang a song that was dedicated to the milkmen of that place, entitled, "Shall We Gather at the River." When he started to sing the boys went out and got a lot of duck eggs and throwed them at him. You ought to have seen him duck eggs.

They have a different way of encoring you down there. They don't clap their hands when they want you to come back. They all holler, "Come back." When we got through they hollered, "Come back! Come back!" One big fellow dared him to come back.

It came my turn next. I said, "Ladies and gentlemen, I will recite you a little poetry. I will take for my subject, "The Lights."

"The lights that shine tonight in this grand theater
 Are not as bright as the lights that shine tonight in
 Denver, Colorata."

They wanted me to sing. I told them I had just received a message saying I had a very bad cold. They insisted I should sing anyhow. I agreed to sing. I said the first part of the song is awfully simple. The second part is simply awful. If you have any tears to shed go to the wood-shed and shed them. When I started to sing I received the greatest ovation of eggs that anybody ever received. I hollered "Fowl!" Before I got half way through the song over half of the audience was on the stage. They said if they could find a rail they would show me a trick. They lifted me up on their shoulders and escorted me to the city limits and told me not to come back and I didn't come back. I kept on going until I got to Fort Smith. When I got there the first place I came to was a saloon. I walked right in and called for a glass of seltzer. The bartender poured it out and set it on the bar. I heard a noise on the outside. I walked to the door to see what it was.

When I came back my seltzer was gone. There was no one there but the bartender and myself; I knew he must have taken it. I hit him. In came a policeman and arrested me. He took me down to the jail, opened up a door and said, "This is your cell, sir."

I found it to be a perfect sell. The windows, they were great. I was just surrounded with bars and couldn't get a drink. United States court is held there for the Indian Territory. All the tough characters are brought there for trial. They usually have a hanging about every Friday. There are a great many people who leave Fort Smith by the rope route. There is a scaffold in the jail yard that accommodates ten at once. The hangman is an old man. He has the distinction of being the champion hangman of the world. He has sprung the trap on eighty-seven men and has shot to death seven. When he gets them on the scaffold he hollers, "Get your feet up even!" When he puts the rope around their necks he tickles them under the chin and tells them he is going to make angels out of them.

While I was in Fort Smith a policeman found a man lying on the sidewalk who had fainted, he took him to the police station. When he got there he discovered the man was dead. They searched him and found a six-shooter and forty dollars. The policeman took the six-shooter; the judge fined him forty dollars for carrying concealed weapons.

———————

Look at the condition of the working man today, where is he? The tinners are continually going up the spout. The plumbers are always in the gutter. The paper-hangers are up against the wall. The bakers are compelled to raise the dough. The police has to be on the beet in order to live. The shoe-makers have to work on their uppers and they get waxed in the end. The clock-makers are run on tick and they are never on time. The old washwoman is always in soak and she is the only one you see hanging out on the line.

———

When I left Fort Smith I remember it was on a Friday night. The 13th day of the month. I had berth 13, and there was a cross-eyed porter on the car. There was a newly married couple in the next berth to me. During the night she wanted a drink of water." She said, "John, get up and get me a drink of water." He said, "Dear, you get up and get it." She said, "How will I know what berth you are in when I come back?" He said, "I will stick my foot out in the aisle." When she came back every man in the car had his foot sticking out in the aisle.

The next morning the porter brushed my clothes. I thanked him.

He said, "Look hyer, boss! You is the sixth man I'se brushed off dis mawnin'; I ain't seen any dust yet."

I said, "There has been over a hundred porters brushed my clothes; none of them ever got any dust out of them."

He said, "You shore carries de dust in your pocket."

The next morning I was riding in the chair car.

There was a fellow sitting along side of me. He seemed to be mighty sleepy. I said, "Did you take a berth last night?" He said, "Yes, but I had an upper berth, and had to get up before I went to bed." I said, "Do you see that scar on my face? That is my berth mark." "How is

ALL FEET LOOKED ALIKE TO HER

that?" "I took a sleeper not long ago and got in the wrong berth."

A boy fell over a lady's valise and said he was just getting over the grip.

There were two brakemen on the train. One was a new man making his first trip. The old brakeman said to the new one, "I will call the station in one end of the car, and you call the

THE SLOW TRAIN ON A DOWN GRADE NIGH LITTLE ROCK,
GWIEN A PERTY GOOD HICKERY

same in the other end." When the train whistled for the station the old brakeman came in and called out the name in the front end of the car.

The new brakeman in the hind end hollered, "The same in this end!" The old brakeman told him the name of the next station and said, "When we get there you call the name in both ends of the car." When the train whistled for the station the new man came in the car. He started to call the station, but had forgotten the name. He stood for a moment, then said, "This is it, people; this is it."

There were several prisoners on the train bound for the states-prison at Little Rock. When we got there we all knew it. The brakeman came in and hollered, "Little Rock! Change clothes. Four years for refreshments. Free conveyance to the state house with all the latest improvements."

When I got off the train I stepped into a hack, and told the driver to take me to a good hotel. He started off with a sudden jerk. After he had drove several blocks I stuck my head out of the door and told him not to drive quite so fast, as I had on a pair of bad shoes. He said, "What has that got to do with me driving fast, you having on a pair of bad shoes?" I told him that when he started the bottom dropped out of the hack and I had been running ever since.

Little Rock is a very interesting place. I started out to see some of the sights. I got on a street car to take a ride. The car was crowded. I was standing up in the aisle holding on to a strap when the car struck a short curve. I fell over on a big, fat lady's lap. She gave me a shove and said, "What are you, a Laplander or a Highlander?" When the conductor came in I saw he was an old friend of mine. I thought I would have a little chat with him. I said, "It is a nice day." He said, "Fair." I had my nickel in my mouth. The car came to a sudden stop and I will be darned if I didn't swallow the nickel. I was in an awful fix. I went to see a doctor. He made me cough up two dollars.

I next visited the Court House. They were trying a fellow for biting off a man's ear. The judge bound him over to keep the piece.

The next one was arrested for stealing a peck measure. The Judge asked him what his business was. He said he was a tailor. The judge said, "You are discharged. If you are a tailor you have a right to take any man's measure."

They brought another fellow in charged with stealing nine bottles of beer. The judge told him he would have to go back and get the other three. He couldn't make a case out of nine.

The next one came up had been fighting. The judge said, "What is your name?" He said, "John Smith." "What is your business?" He said he was a locksmith. The judge said, "Ten dollars. Locksmith up."

A policeman brought in three Chinamen and an Irishman. The Chinamen had been smoking opium. The Irishman was booked for getting drunk and disturbing the peace. The judge said to the first Chinaman, "What is your name?" He said, "Ah Sin." "Thirty days." He said to the next Chinaman, "What is your name?" He said, "Ah Chung." "Thirty days." He said to the next Chinaman, "What is your name?" He said, "Ah Bung." "Thirty days." The judge said to the

Irishman, "What is you name?" He said, "Ah Hell, I suppose it is thirty days anyhow."

I think a married woman should take her name from the position her husband holds in life. You take a baker's wife; she should be called Dora. A shoemaker's wife should be called Peggie. A street car conductor's wife you would call her Carrie. A breweryman, he should have a wife with a cork leg; then he would get his hops for nothing. When I marry I am going to call my wife muskmellon, then she cantaloupe.

I had an old friend living in Little Rock by the name of Work. I started out to find him. I was standing on the street corner. A policeman asked me what I was waiting for. I told him I was looking for Work. He said, "If you are looking for work go down to the City Hall and you can get a job sweeping the streets if you are out for the dust." I called him a lobster, then he pinched me.

I saw some funny things happen while I was in Little Rock. I saw a runaway team come down the street. It ran into a butcher wagon and knocked the liver right out of it. Saw a fellow drive a team over a man. After he got over him he stopped and hollered, "Look out!" The fellow said, "What's the matter? Are you coming back again?" I saw a fellow running down the street. A policeman stopped him and asked him if he was training for a race. He said, "No, he was racing for a train."

Little Rock is noted for pretty girls. I met one of the first girls of the town. That is, the first as you drive in.   Her name was Auto.   I think she was from Mobile.   There was one thing about her I didn't like.   That was her feet.   They were just as long behind as they were in front.   You couldn't tell which way she was going.   She was the most bashful girl I ever saw.   She wouldn't go by a

THE BASHFUL GIRL

lumber yard where there was undressed lumber. She wouldn't even wear a watch because it had hands.   She wouldn't look at a band playing where they had a bass drum.   She said she wouldn't stand and see any man beat his bearskin.   She wouldn't wear undressed kids.   She even had pants made for the table legs.   We were out one evening and she exposed her ignorance.   We went into where there was a soda water fountain.   I called for an egg phosphate. She said she would take hers scrambled. We went to the theater. We were sitting up in the gallery, a fellow came out on the stage and began to roll up a carpet. All the boys began to holler "Supe!" She said, "They are hollering 'soup,' let's go down and get some." After the show I took her home. We started to play cards. She held hearts and I held diamonds. Her father came in. He wanted a hand. He held clubs. I begged, he gave me one right across the head and knocked me through the window. I sashed right through. I took panes as I went out; I went right by the way of Glasgow. I asked the old man if he didn't have a full hand. He said "Why, so?" I said, "It beat me."

Speaking of love. There is an object lesson shown in making love. Very few know the true art of making love. The way a young man should make love to his girl is like this: He should drop down on his knees before her and say:

"My Josafine, my Kerosine, my Gasoline, my Benzine, my Vaseline, I come from above my station without hesitation or preservation to ask you to become my relation so as to increase the population in this great nation."

CONUNDRUMS.

Did you ever hear the story about the dirty window.

No. What is it?

No use to tell it; you couldn't see through it.

What is the best thing to tell a woman?

Nothing.

It's all over the house.

WHAT YOU SEE IN THE HILLS OF ARKANSAW

What?
The roof.
What is the best way to make a slow horse fast?
Tie him to a post.
Johnson got arrested for stealing a pig.
How did they know he stole it?
The pig squealed on him.
That sticks you.
What?
Pin.   .
That lets you out.
What?
The door.

_____

I was invited to a party.   I remember they played several games, one they call, "Heavy, heavy hangs over your head."   Some one hung a baseball bat over my head.   They played a game called pins and needles.   There is a game you can get stuck at every time.   You can get lots of pointers.   They played a game called "Kissen."

Did you ever play that game?   To kiss a young lady it costs you fifty cents.   To kiss a married lady it costs twenty-five cents.   Old maids three for ten.   Then we played that game called Christmas.   That is where everybody hangs up their stockings.   The first stocking belonged to a young lady from Boston.   She got in her stockings two lead pencils, and, strange to say, they just fit.   The next was a young lady from Cincinnati.   She got in her stockings a bushel of potatoes.   Strange to say, it just fit.   The next was a young lady from St. Louis.   She got in her stockings a barrel of flour, and, strange to say, it just fit.   The next one belonged

to a Little Rock girl.   She got in her stockings a
ton of coal, and strange to say, it just fit.   Next
came me.   I didn't know they were going to play
that game.   I didn't have on any stockings, so
I hung up my pants.   I must have got a man in
them, for I had to go home in a barrel, and I think
they just fit, for I haven't seen them since.

Everybody had to recite a piece of poetry.   The
first one started off something like this:

> " 'Tis sweet to see a bumble-bee
>   When ere you go a fishing,
> But if you sit right down on him,
>   He will change your disposition."

And the next one:

> "The rose is red, the violet's blue,
>   Where you see three balls you will see a Jew."

The next took a young lady for a subject and said:

> "Young lady enters car,
>   Ten men stands up, and thar you are."

The next one took an old maid for a subject:

> "Old maid enters car,
>   Nary man stands up, and thar you are."

It came my turn next.   I said:

> "Whenever I marry it will not be for love or riches,
>   But I'll marry a girl that is six feet tall so she can wear the
>   breeches."

I met the Little family while I was down there.
There is Mr. Little and Mrs. Little, and they have
five children.   Mr. Little only gets four dollars a
week, and I asked him how he managed to keep
such a large family on such a small salary, and
he said every Little helped.

I had an old friend living in Little Rock by the
name of Burnside.   They said he lived over on the
North side.   I went over to the North side to see

Burnside. When I got over to the North side they said Burnside had moved to the Southside. When I got to the South side they said he had gone to the West side. When I got to the West side they said he had gone over to the East side. I went over to the East side, they told me he had gone back to the North side. I went to where he did reside and knocked on the outside. They opened the door on the inside, I inquired for Burnside. They said he he had died. Then I cried. That's about all I know about Burnside.

Me and your brother and another fellow were choosing the other day what kind of wife we would like to have in case we got married. Your brother said when he got married he wanted a wife that was like a Bible.

Why did he want a wife like a Bible?

Because she would be seldom looked at.

The other fellow said he wanted a wife that was like a piano.

Why did he want a wife like a piano?

Because she would be upright and grand.

I said when I got married I wanted a wife that was like an almanac.

Why did you want a wife like an almanac?

Because I could get a new one every year.

How is your brother, the one we used to call Sponge? The reason we called him Sponge, he used to be all the time soaked.

How is your brother, the one that steals?

I want you to understand, sir, that my brother don't steal.

Yes he does steal, and I can prove it.

Well, then, prove it.

The other night me and your brother was invited down to the festival. We were awful hungry; your brother was so hungry he couldn't wait; at exactly sixty minutes past seven he eight a clock. All the nice silverware was spread out on the table. Your brother stole a spoon and put it in his boot. They kept watching so I couldn't get any; determined not

AT THE CIRCUS

to be outdone by your brother, I picked up a spoon, held it up in my hands and said, "Ladies and gentlemen, I will show you a trick." I put the spoon in my inside pocket and said, "Now you will find it over there in that nigger's boot." They caught your brother and took the spoon away from him.

There was a circus in town while I was there. I took my girl and went out to see it. All the boys and girls were there. I saw one fellow take his girl up to a lemonade stand and buy one glass of red lemonade. He drank half of it, passed it over to his girl she drank the other half. I saw another fellow and his girl. He bought one dish of ice cream and got two spoons. When we came to the elephant my girl asked me what that big thing was hanging down in front. I said, "That is his trunk." She said, "It is a wonder he wouldn't open it and put on a clean shirt." She said, "If that big thing in front is his trunk, that little thing behind (meaning his tail), must be his valise." There was a lady and a little boy right next to me. When they got to the cage where the baboon was the little boy said, "Oh, mamma, look at papa." When I came out a messenger boy came up to me and said he was looking for L. E. Fant. I told him there were several L. E. Fants in the tent.

When the circus got ready to leave town the railroad company refused to take the elephants because they could not get their trunks checked.

I was standing on the street corner. There was a funeral procession going by. It was an awful long procession. There must have been at least fifty carriages in line. There was a couple of railroad men standing along side of me. One was a brakeman the other an engineer. The brakeman said to the engineer, "Who is dead? It must be some prominent person." The engineer said, "No, it is just a railroad man." He said, "It must be an official then." The engineer said, "No, it is just one of our engineers." The brakeman said, "Well, if he ever looks back and sees all that string behind him he will double into the cemetery."

I met an old friend of mine I hadn't seen for a good many years. We used to be boys together. It was indeed a pleasure to talk of old times. When we used to go out in the fields and see the grasshoppers making grass, and see the butterflies making butter, see the caterpillars making cats and watch the bumble bees making bums. He said, "Don't you remember when you used to come by the old village blacksmith shop and see me there shooing flies?" I said, "Yes, don't you remember when we used to go out and make mud pies and you used to eat 'em?" I remember when we went to school the boys used to call you big head. You came in the house one day crying and told the teacher the boys had been calling you big head. She said, "I wouldn't mind that, Willie, there is nothing in it."

My friend looked as though he had seen better days. He looked as though liquor had gotten the best of him. I asked him in to have a drink with me. We ordered our drinks. He poured his out and held it up in his hand and said:

"This is what makes me wear old clothes,
    Lie, beg and steal;
Get out in the street and much a meal;
Dig down in my pocket and spend my last dime,
And wear my summer clothes in the winter time."

After we had talked over old times for a few minutes he said, "Well, have one with me." We called for another drink; he threw a dollar on the bar and said:

"Bright silver dollar, gleaming there all alone,
All your boon companions have been spent and gone.
The most useful money ever issued, that is true;
All the rest has gone for liquor, so I will just spend you."

Me and my friend walked out and were strolling leisurely along the street when the fire bell rang.

People ran pell-mell from all directions. The fire engine came tearing down the street. Only a short distance away we saw a large building all in flames. We rushed to the spot. I heard a scream; I looked up and saw standing in a window a young girl wringing her hands and begging to be saved. Every avenue of escape was gone. I was horrified. I fell back dumbfounded and stared; my friend he stared; that made a pair of stairers; the girl walked down the stairs and went home.

When I left Little Rock my next stop was Hot Springs. We made pretty good time on that road. The waiter came in and hollered, "First and last call for dinner in the dining car! The first car in the rear. The only car. All those wishing to shake hands with the knife and fork will please walk back!" I proceeded to the dinner. There was a fellow sitting at the table with me. It was very evident from the way he acted he hadn't been accustomed to eating in a dining car. I looked over the bill of fare. The waiter asked me what I would have. I said, "Immaterial." He said he would take the same. A fellow sitting at the next table ordered turkey. When the waiter brought it in he was carrying it on a tray filled with dishes. The train struck a sharp curve. He slipped and fell and broke all the dishes. The colored waiter was lying on the floor. The conductor said, "Look here, sir, you have created an international disturbance. This is the downfall of Africa, the spilling of Greece, the overthrow of Turkey and the breaking up of China." The waiter began to cry. He said it was the first time he ever had a tray full beat.

The waiter brought me a steak. It was so tough

I couldn't stick my fork in the gravy.   I held it up and said:

"Old ox, old ox! How came you here?
You have plowed the fields for many a year.
You have been kicked and cuffed with great abuse,
And now brought here for the railroad's use."

There was a gambler on the train.   He was a full-fledged gambler.   He wanted to bet with everybody.   He wanted to bet with me.   He said, "I will

BIG WRECK

bet you this train gets in late."   I told him no, I wouldn't bet.   He said, "I bet you it gets in ahead of time."   I said, "No!"   Then he said, "I bet you it don't get in at all."   We ran a little way further and had a big wreck.   The car we were in was smashed all to pieces.   I went up in the air about fifty feet. When I was coming down I met the gambler going up with his valise in his hand. When he passed me he said, "I bet you five dollars I go higher than you did."

I had heard a great deal about Hot Springs before I got there. Most everybody has heard of Hot Springs. That is a great place to go and get cured of rheumatism. Most everybody that comes to Hot Springs is a cripple in some way or the other. I never saw so many crippled people in my life. Twisted arms and legs. I met a cross-eyed man. He looked crooked. I imagined I was in Cripple Creek. At the hotel I stopped at they told me they hadn't bought any wood for ten years. The cripples that had come there and been cured had left crutches enough to keep them in wood.

I was sick while I was there. I couldn't eat anything. After I had gone to every house in town they wouldn't let me eat. A particular friend of mine came to me and advised me to leave town. He was the chief of police. I felt so bad I went to see a doctor. He said, "Do you want to be treated?" I said, "Yes. That is, if you have it here in the office." He said, "You don't understand me. I will examine you thoroughly for twenty dollars." I said, "All right, go ahead, but if you find it I want ten of it." After he had examined me he said, "You want to get glasses and wear them." I went down to a place where they use glasses. I'd taken three, I believe it was, when I'd started out. A fellow said, "Have another one with me." I did and felt better, too. The next day I felt sick again. Went to see another doctor. He asked me what I had been eating. I told him, "Nothing, only some honey." He said, "You have got the hives."

HOT SPRINGS, ARK.

He would have been a good doctor but he didn't have the patients. He told me that I would have to take something. He said, "Go take something right away." I went down the street. I saw a drunken man. I took his watch. That was about all he had with him. They had me arrested. When they caught me the watch was still going. I went to see a lawyer. He got the case; I got the works.

Hot Springs is a very warm place. You hear everybody talk about coming there to get boiled out. There is nothing under a hundred in the shade that would interest a man there at all. The word zero is unknown. It is so hot there in the summer time the hens lay hard boiled eggs. I had a dream down there. Dreamt I died, then the heat woke me up. There are some peculiar things about the climate there. You can't raise water melons. The vines grow so fast it wears the little ones off on the ground. I went out with a fellow to plant cucumbers. The first thing I knew I was all tangled up in the vines. Ran my hand in my pocket to get a knife to cut the vines and pulled out a cucumber a foot long.

I was arrested for carrying concealed weapons. They took me before the judge and searched me. All they found was a yeast cake. They fined me ten dollars. I said, "Judge, that isn't concealed weapons." He said, "It's a kind of a raiser." I said "Give me the yeast cake and I will go out and see if I can raise the dough."

I couldn't make the raise, so I wrote home for money. I said:

Dear Father:

Roses are red, violets are blue,
Send me ten dollars and I will owe you.

The answer came something like this:

Roses are red, roses are pink,
Inclosed you will find ten dollars, I don't think.

They brought in a colored fellow for cutting another colored man. The judge said, "What did you cut that man for?" He said, "I tell you, judge, he had been sayin' some things 'bout me; when I axed him 'bout it he said he was a hot coon from Cynthy, but when I slit him up de back wif my rahzar I don't think he was so warm." The judge said, "A little louder." He said, "Yo heerd me." The judge said, "Six months." He said, "What's that?" The judge said, "You heard me."

They next brought in a tramp. He had been arrested for sleeping in a coal house. The judge asked him if he didn't find that a pretty hard bed. He said no, it was soft coal. The judge said, "What is your business?" He said he was a rough rider. The judge said, "Where did you ever do any rough riding?" He said on the Missouri & Pacific railroad. The judge asked him if he ever worked. He said once. "What did you do?" He said he "layed over a skylight to keep the sun out." "Who are you?" "My father was a hero, my mother was a shero, and I am a hobo." The judge said, "I sentenced you to jail for thirty days for setting fire to a rock quarry." He said, "I refuse to go. Bring the jail to me."

I received a letter from a cousin of mine in Klondike. It read something like this:

                                     Klondike, Septuber,
The 17th.   Soktober, No Vonder,

My Dear Cousin:—

· I take my pen in hand to let you know that we don't live where we did, but we live where we have moved. Your uncle, whom you love so well, is dead. Hoping this will find you just the same. When he died he left you $15,000. We will send it to you just as quick as we can find it. He also willed you $50,000 you are to get when Dawson City dies. They don't know the cause of his death, only that all of his breath leaked out. The doctor gave up all hopes of saving him when he died. Your aunt is also dead. When she died she left $50,000 sewed up in her bustle. What a lot of money to leave behind. We have all got the mumps, we are having a swell time. I sent you your black overcoat, and to save the express charges I cut off the buttons. You will find them in the inside pocket. Mother is making sausages. All the neighbors are looking for their dogs. Father is not in the pocket-book business any more. He has gone into the stocking business. They say there is more money in stockings these days than pocket books. Your girl, whom you thought was dead and in Heaven, is alive and in Hell-ene, Montana. Her father said if you don't send him that forty cents you owe him he will scratch your nails out with his eyes. The Damn family is still living at the same old place. Old man Damn is sick. The old lady Damn is also sick. The whole Damn family is sick. As I have nothing more to write I will close—my face.

P. S.—If you don't get this let me know and I will write again.

A coon that has lost his home, in other words, his meal ticket. He goes up and knocks on his girl's door.

She says, "Who's dar?"

"It's me honey."

"Who's me?"

"It's yo' Charlie. Com open de door, hun."

"What do yo' want?"

A COON THAT HAS LOST HIS HOME

"I just want to tell yo' how much I luv's yo'."

"Yo' had better tell it through de door den, fo' **I'se** done **got** a good job cooking fo' de white folks.

I gets three dollars a week. I ain't gwine to 'low yo' to com between me and my work."

"Say, honey, let me in. It's cold out here, and it's snowin'."

"Yo' knowed it was cold befo' yo' went out dar. I tole yo' 'way long last summer when yo' was layin' round here dat winter was comin' on."

"Say, honey, if yo' will just let me in I will git a job and I'll work all de time."

"Niggah, I'se done tole yo' I wasn't gwine to let yo' sip'rate me from my work."

"Just stick yo' head over de transom den, and let me tell yo' how much I luv's yo'."

"I ain't gwine to stick my head out at no transom, for I knows yo' is fixin' to bounce a rock on it."

"I tell yo' it is cold out here, and I wants in."

"If it is too cold out dar yo' had better make some 'rangements wif de wedder."

"Look here now, I'se gittin' mad. If yo' don't open dat door I'se gwine to kick it down."

Another nigger on the inside says, "Say, Liza, gimme my hat. I'se gwine to go."

"What yo' want to go for? It ain't nobody but Charlie, and yo' is twice as big as him."

"Yes, but Charlie carries de diffunce 'round in his pocket."

"Yo' better not jump out of dat window, niggah. Dar's a bull dog in dat back yard."

"I doan' care if dar's a yard full of bull dogs."

"Why doan' yo' go out de front way? Dar's no-body out dar but Charlie, and he's only one."

"Yo' ain't counted Charlie lately."

"Go on out de front way. Charlie ain't gwine to bodder yo'."

"If I go out de front way de'll be walkin' slow behind me tomorrow."

"Look here, if yo' doan open this door I'll kick it down, and I'll bust de nose off yo' face."

"I bet if yo' do, yo' will run ever' time yo' sees a nose, and yo' will run so fas' yo' ankles 'll git so hot dey will burn yo' legs up."

I was walking up the street. I heard a little bird singing. I said to myself, "That little bird is singing for me." A fellow behind me said it was singing for him. I said, "No, it is singing for me." He hit me and I hit him. A policeman arrested us; took us up before the judge. He asked me what I had to say. I said I was walking up the street and I heard a little bird singing. I said it was singing for me. He said it was singing for him. He hit me and I hit him. The judge said, "Ten dollars each. It wasn't singing for either one of you. It was singing for me."

I just had five dollars left; went in a restaurant; bought a five dollar meal ticket; came out on the sidewalk; was counting up how many meals I could eat when the fire bell rang. A big fellow ran against me; knocked my meal ticket down on the sidewalk and stepped on it. He had nails in his boots and punched out four dollars and eighty cents.

I was walking up the street. Saw a basket of eggs setting in front of a store. I never wanted an egg so bad in my life. I picked up an egg and started up the street. The man that owned the egg saw me, and was coming right behind me. Didn't want him to catch me with the egg, so I put it in my mouth.

He walked up and slapped me on the back. Well, I'll be darned if I didn't swallow the egg. I was in an awful fix. I was afraid to move around for fear the egg would break. I was afraid to stand still for fear it would hatch.

I went to church. Just as they arose to sing the closing hymn somebody hollered fire. In the excitement I jumped out of a window and was arrested for making a dive out of a church.

A gambler went into a pawn shop to borrow some money. He was well acquainted with the Jew that ran the place. He told the Jew he would like to borrow fifty dollars for a few days and would give him his note. He let him have the money. When the note became due the gambler went in and told him that he had been playing in some hard luck and didn't have the money at present, but would have it in a few days and would come around and pay him. The Jew said, "Vell, I haf your note, I vant my money." The fellow said, "I haven't got it. I can't pay you until I get it." The Jew said, "Vell, but I haf your note. I vant my money. Here vas your note." The fellow got mad, pulled out a pistol pointed it at the Jew's head, and said, "You eat that note or I will kill you." The Jew ate the note. In a few days the gambler got the money; came around and paid him. The Jew said, "You vas a good fellow, you vas all right. Whenever you vant any more money come to me." In a few days the fellow wanted to borrow some more money. He came to the Jew; told him he would like to give his note for fifty dollars for a few days. He said, all right. He started to write it out. The Jew said,

"Mine friend, vait a minute. Vould you just as soon write it on a ginger snap?"

I saw a fellow hit a Jew and knock him down. The Jew got up and said, "Do it again." The fellow knocked him down again. The Jew got up and said,

HE SAID 'HIT ME AGAIN"

"Do it again." The fellow knocked him down again. A policeman came up and arrested them. He said to the Jew, "What did you want that fellow to keep knocking you down for?" The Jew said, "Because every time he hit me I saw a diamond."

I saw many comical things among the colored people in Hot Springs. I was strolling through the suburbs of the town one day and I heard an old colored woman say, "Look here, 'Liza, you better come away from that straw stack you will git de hay fever. Cum in de house and scum dem 'lasses, yo'.

A WAY DOWN SOUTH

better not spill any either. If yo' does I'll stomp yo' in de ground

"Look heah, you George Washington, what I done already tole you 'bout being round heah Sunday mawnin' bar futed? Chile, yo' know don't who yo' is named aftah. Yo' Authur cum heah and quit yo' playing wid dem poor white trash. Dey lick de 'lasses off your hand den call yo' nigger."

There was a young colored fellow coming down the street. He had just got a new watch. He saw another colored fellow he knew coming. He wanted the other fellow to know he had a new watch. The other fellow said to him, "Whar is yo' gwine?" "Whar is I gwine? I'se gwine just whar I'se gwine, dat whar I'se gwine. Ef yo' wants a watch, go buy yo'se'f a watch and doan' cum foolin' wid a gentleman on de street." "Look hare. Yo' better hush up and quit yo' foolin' and go on. De fust ting yo' knows I'se gwine to cut yo' to de fat."

I overheard a conversation between two old colored ladies that met on the street going in opposite directions. Neither one stopped. They said: "Good evenin', Mrs. Jones." "Good evenin', Mrs. Brown." "How's all yo' folks?" "All our folks is well 'cept Sam and Sam he's got de lumbago." "De lumbago? De good God. Che-he-he-ha-ha-hah. Yo' all cum down sometime." "We will, thank yo'. Yo' all cum down too." "Bough-hu-wah-hah-ge he he he."

Down there the colored people have a new way of learning their children at school. They just say, "Ta-rar-rar-da-boom-de-a. Ta-rar-rar-da-boom-de-b. Ta-rar-rar-da-boom-de-c. Ta-rar-rar-da-boom-de-d."

I met a colored man there from Chicago. He said he didn't like it down south. He said the people there let you know you are colored. He said in Chicago you don't know you are colored unless you look in the glass.

I was sitting in front of a hotel when an old man drove up and asked the landlord if he wanted to buy some fresh country butter. He said, "Wait a minute and I will ask my wife." He went to the telephone and asked his wife if she wanted to buy some butter. When he came back the old man said, " I know I look pretty green, but if you think you can make me believe your wife is in that little box you are badly mistaken."

I saw a tramp go up to a house and knock on the door. When the lady opened the door the tramp asked her if she would give him something to eat. She brought out some dry bread and told him that was all she had and would give it to him for God's sake. He asked her if she wouldn't " Put some butter on it for Christ's sake."

I stopped at a place where they were raising a subscription for the purpose of fencing in a cemetery. Every one had donated very liberally except one fellow. He was opposed to fencing it in for two reasons. He said, " In the first place there was no one in the graveyard that could get out; in the second place there was no one out that wanted to get in."

There was a stuttering man running a blacksmith shop. Another stuttering man went into the shop who wanted to learn the blacksmith trade. The blacksmith heated a horse shoe red hot   He told the other stuttering fellow to hit it. He said, " Wha-wha-wha-wha-wha-when- nau - nau - nau - nau - now?" The blacksmith said, " Nau-nau-nau-nau-nau-not-now. It-it-it-is-is-is-co-co-co-cold."

Dr. Brown went out in the country. He fell in a well and was drowned. They got him out and brought him back to town. The people didn't show him a bit of sympathy. They said he ought to have been attending to the sick, and let the well alone.

While I was down there a fellow accused me of stealing his shirt and pawning it. "Yes," he said, "you stole my shirt and pawned it." I said, "No, I didn't steal your shirt and pawn it, and I can prove it." He said, "Well, then prove it." I unbuttoned my vest and showed him his shirt, and I proved to him I hadn't pawned it.

It is remarkable how many shirts you can get out of one yard, providing you get in the right yard.

"I was down by your house today."

"Why didn't you come in?"

"I would, only I didn't know where you lived."

"I met you on the street today."

"Why didn't you speak to me?"

"I would, but I didn't know you."

"Who was that lady I saw you with?"

"That wasn't a lady, that was my wife."

"I never see you any more, where do you keep yourself?"

"Up at the butcher shop."

"There ain't no fun at the butcher shop."

"They are all the time cutting up."

"How is your wife?"

"She's in good spirits."

"She is?"

"Yes, she's dead."

"I thought you just said she was in good spirits?"

"She is. She's preserved in alcohol."

"How is your wife?"

"She is sick lying at death's door. I went to see

a doctor; he said he thought he could pull her through."

"Have you any children?"

"Five."

"All living?"

"Three are."

"Where are the other two?"

"They are in Omaha."

"Have you any children?"

"One cute little boy, and he looks just like me."

"Well, I wouldn't let that worry me, if I was you. The boy can't help it. Probably he will grow over it."

"Do you remember that little dog of mine? He is dead."

"I suppose he died the same old way, swallowed a tape line and died by inches?"

"Oh, no. He went up the alley and died by the yard."

"There has been a remarkable thing happened up in our neighborhood. A little baby gained fifteen pounds in three weeks."

"That isn't anything remarkable. Up in our neighborhood a baby gained seventy-five pounds in three weeks."

"That was remarkable."

"What did they feed that baby on?"

"Elephant's milk."

"Who did the baby belong to?"

"The elephant."

"Do you know that in San Francisco there is a doctor that raises babies in an incubator? Isn't that a wonderful invention? Just think of it, raising babies in an incubator."

"Yes, just think of it.   How would you like to have to say your mother was an oil stove?"

"Speaking of inventions, some of the large cities of the east have adopted a new method of sweeping the streets.   They use ladies' corsets.   They say that they gather in the waste better."

"I see by the papers that there has been a corset trust formed.   That's a trust you can't bust.   It has come to stay and it will squeeze the people."

Speaking of trusts.   There is the beef trust; they say it's a bully thing but we should steer clear of it. They have raised the price of meat until it's getting so a working man can't eat meat; the nearest he can come to eating meat is oxtail soup and beef tongue; that is the only way he can make both ends meet.

The working man will have to economize.   He should let his wife do the cooking, then he won't eat half so much.

Just the other day my wife went downtown and paid twenty dollars for an embroidered handker-chief.   I told her that twenty dollars was too much to blow in.

"I saw a terrible thing happen as I was coming down the street today.   A trolley wire came down and fell across a horse's neck and killed him instantly."

"That's nothing.   I was coming down the street the other day, seven trolley wires came down and fell across my neck and didn't kill me."

"Didn't you know that rubber was a non-conductor?"

"I suppose you have traveled a good deal?"

"Yes all over the world.   I crossed the dead sea before it died."

"Have you ever been to Turkey?"

"Yes."

"How did you like Turkey?"

"Stuffed with oysters."

"Have you ever been to China?"

"Yes, I just went over to Peek-in."

"Tell me something of China."

"Do you know that in China they take all the little baby girls out in the middle of the river in a boat and throw them overboard and let the lobsters get them? It is different in this country. They wait till they grow up. Then the lobsters get them."

I have a brother that looks just like me. We look so much alike you can't tell one from the other. He had a job down town working in a big store. He started in at the bottom of the ladder. He worked himself up round by round. When he reached the top of the ladder they gave him the windows to wash. He didn't like that job, so he quit. He started out to hunt another job. He went to a place and asked a man for a job. The man said, "I want to see how much you know. I will just ask you three questions. If you answer them I will give you a job. The first question is, how many corners has the moon got?" He couldn't answer that one. Then he said, "How many stars are there?" He couldn't answer that. Then he said, "What am I thinking about?" He didn't know that one either. Then he said, "I will give you until 10 o'clock tomorrow to study on those questions. If you come back then and answer them, I will give you the job." He said, "All right." He came home and told me about it. I said, "I have got an idea. We look so much alike he can't tell us apart. I will go down there and answer the questions. He will think it's you, and I will get the job. He said, "All right." Next day I went down. He said, "Have you come to answer the questions?" I said, "Yes." He said, "The first question is, how many corners has the moon got?" I said, "Six." I knew he didn't know, so he had to take my word for it. He said, "How many stars are there?" I said, "Four hundred and seventy-five million, six hundred and eighty-three thousand, seven hundred and sixty-five. If you don't believe me, go out and count them yourself." Of course he didn't want to do that. He said, "This is the last one. I guess I have got you now. What am I thinking about?" I said, "You think you are talking to my brother, but you ain't." I got the job. My brother looks so much like me I put my money in his pocket.

While walking along the street today I saw what I call a disgusting sight; it was a woman that had fallen so low as to come upon the public thoroughfare wearing a motherhubbard with the four corners blowing to the wind. Just think of a woman having no more pride and self respect for herself than to come upon the street wearing a motherhubbard. I never struck a woman in my life but if I should ever catch my wife on the street wearing a motherhubbard, I think I would walk up to her and give her a belt.

Women are very peculiar. You never can understand them. Not long ago I went home. My wife was gone and the door was locked. I went down through the coal hole and up through the cellar, got a ladder and crawled through the transom, found a note on the table from my wife saying I would find the key under the mat on the front door step.

My wife is a lovely cook. I have eaten several of her dishes, such as cold shoulder and hot tongue. She can't stand flattery though. I called her honey. The next day she thought she had the hives.

WEARING A MOTHER-HUBBARD ON THE STREET

The other day I was out in the alley and found a twenty dollar gold piece. I came home and told my wife about it. Now she is suing me for a divorce and alley-money.

You take a woman and she will go around town all day. She comes home in time to get the supper. She has a lot of samples to show you. You take a man when he has been around town all day, he comes home in the evening, just look at the samples he will bring.   That is about the only time his wife wants to kiss him.   She wants to see what kind of samples he has been getting.

Women go to the theaters night after night just to see what the other women wear.   It is different with the men.   They go there just to see what they don't wear.

I think women would make better soldiers than men.   They are more used to powder.   One woman told me she just used a little bit to keep away the chaps.   I think it is just to draw them on.

You take the women, they are always talking about the men.

If you see two or three women talking on the street corner they are talking about the men.

· I went to church last Sunday.   All the young ladies in the choir sang, "Only for a mansion in the sky."   That shun in the sky was all a bluff.   All they wanted was the man.   When they got through all the old maids said, "A-man."

When a girl laughs she always says "He-he-he." You never saw a man laugh and say, "She-she-she."

Speaking of women.   Boys let me give you a little advice,   never marry a harness-maker's daughter for you never know how sadly will be your fate until you have been led to the halter.   If you try to hold a tight rein on her something may come upon the spur of the moment and you would get bit.   She may be a little sulky, her bed may be a little buggy, and she may have a wagen tongue.   She may not be well spoken of.   Other fellows may spring up and you would soon tire of that.

Whenever I go down town in the evening I always make it a point to get home at a reasonable hour so as not to keep my wife up late.   The last evening I was down town I took home an awful big load.   I think it was the biggest load I ever carried and I have carried some pretty big loads.   When I got home my wife met me at the door and said, "What time is it?"   I said, "Just eleven o'clock." Just then the old clock struck two.   She said, "You have lied to me.   You told me it was eleven o'clock and the old family clock has contradicted you.   It has struck two and proved to me that you have lied. Ain't you ashamed of yourself?   To come home this time of the night drunk and lie to your poor wife like this?   Yes, sir, you have lied to me.   The old clock has proven to me that you have lied."   I couldn't stand it any longer.   I commenced to cry. . I said, "I'm not crying because you have scolded me.   It is not because I have come home drunk.   It is not because my conscience hurts me.   We have been married nigh on to fifteen years.   I have always been a good, kind and loving husband, and to think after all I have done for you, you believe an old three dollar clock before you would your husband."

We have got a boy.   His name is Harry.   He don't mind very well.   The other day his mother started to whip him.   He ran out in the yard and crawled under the house.   She went out and tried to coax him to come out.   She told me about it.   I went out and crawled under the house to get him to come out. He looked at me and said, "What's the matter, papa, is mamma after you too?"

My wife sent our boy down to the butcher shop to see if the butcher had pig's feet.   He came home and told his mother he couldn't tell, as the butcher had on his shoes.

I went down to the butcher shop, called for ten cents' worth of dog meat. The butcher looked at me and said, "Shall I wrap it up, or do you want to eat it here?"

"What was all that old scrap iron I saw you wearing the other day?"

"That was the medals I got for being in the war."

"This government don't give medals for running."

"I fought all through the war."

"I was shot in the head over twenty years ago. It was only yesterday I was seized with a severe spell of coughing and coughed up the bullet."

"You say you were shot in the head over twenty years ago and coughed up the bullet yesterday?"

"Yes, sir."

"That goes to show me how long it takes anything to go through your head."

"It is the first time I ever heard of your coughing up anything."

"I was all through the war. I was at the battle of Santiago. I was first sturgeon."

"You mean first sergeant."

"I was one of the brave soldiers. I was what they call a picket soldier. I was doing picketing. I picked so many chickens I was afraid to go to bed at night. I was afraid I would lay there. While I was fighting at the battle of Santiago fifteen balls pierced my manly bosom."

"And didn't kill you?"

"No."

"How was that?"

"They were codfish balls. One ball went right through me and killed another man. They had me arrested for murder. They said it was through me the other man got killed. I was where the bullets were the thickest. They were just rolling all over me. There was a hole in the bottom of the ammunition wagon."

"Supposing you had seen the enemy coming towards you, would you have formed a line?"

"Yes, I would have drawn a line, a bee line for home."

"In France the soldiers all wear armor for protection to save their lives. In this country Armour killed all of our soldiers."

"What is you business?"

"I am a Life Saver."

"I would like you to tell me of a case where you ever saved any lives."

"Only a short time ago I was strolling along the beach at Boston, picking up a few shells."

"Did you pick up the right one?"

"I saw coming toward me three people. They had their hands in their pockets."

"They were onto you."

"Presently I looked out into the Bay, just as I did I saw a boat capsize. I saw the people struggling in the water. I swam out and rescued them one by one. When I had brought the last one, a lady, safely to shore, I looked out in the Bay and saw floating on top of the water what looked to me to be a lady's head. I swam out to it, and to my surprise it was a lady's switch. I brought it to shore and handed it to the lady. She thanked me."

"So you say you are a life saver. I would call you a hair restorer."

"Do you remember old Deacon Jones? He is still living. Do you remember his son Abe? He was a good-for-nothing sort of fellow. Abe gave the old man a great deal of trouble. The deacon got terrible

THE PREACHERS

mad at Abe one day and told him to leave the house and never come back. Yes, he told him to go to the real place. He said, 'Go down there and never come back.' Abe went away. They never heard anything more from him until one night last winter. The deacon had invited all the preachers in the surrounding country to the house. It was a bitter cold night. All the preachers were sitting around the stove when they heard a knock at the door. The deacon got up and went to the door and there stood poor Abe, cold and shivering. The deacon said,

'Where have you been?' He said, 'Where you told me, down there.' 'How did you find things down there?' 'Just like they are here at home, so many preachers there I couldn't get to the fire.'

CONUNDRUMS.

Did you ever hear the story about the mountain? No, I never did. It's all bluff.

Did you ever hear the story about the cliff? It's just bluff.

How is the best way to keep friends? Treat them kindly? No, often.

How is the best way to find a man out. Go to his house when he ain't at home.

Why is a kiss over a telephone like a straw hat? Because it isn't felt.

If you were hungry where would you go to get something to eat? To the Sandwich Islands.

If the ice wagon weighs two thousand pounds, what does the man on the hind end of the wagon weigh? He weighs ice.

Suppose you were out in the middle of the river in a boat, you had a box of cigars and you wanted to smoke, you didn't have any matches, what would you do for a light? I would take a cigar out of the box, that would make the box a cigar lighter.

Do you know that the United States has a lot of relations? England is the mother, George Washington is the father, New Jersey is an Aunt, Carry Nation is another relation to this great nation.

Scotland grows the thistle,
England grows the rose,
Ireland grows the shamrock,
And the Sheney grows the nose.

I am in a good business now; I am in the chicken business. At first I fed my chickens on cornmeal and sawdust. They done fine, in fact they done so well I cut out the cornmeal altogether and just fed them on sawdust. Then they didn't do so well; one hen laid a knot-hole; another laid a two-inch board; I thought they were going to lay out a whole set of furniture. Every time I tried to eat any of the eggs I would get my mouth full of splinters.

My brother he is very lucky. He was going down the street and fell in a coal hole. He sued the city for ten thousand dollars, and got it. I was going down the street; I fell in a coal hole; got arrested for stealing coal.

"Did you ever go to school?"

"Yes."

"I use to go to High School. The one upon the hill."

"What branches did you study?"

"Most all of them. Hickory, ash and walnut."

"What class was you in?"

"I was in the B class. The reason they put me in the B class was because I had the hives."

"I will see how you are on spelling. Spell 'Blind Pig.'"

"B-l-i-n-d p-g."

"Why did you leave the 'I' out?"

"Because the pig was blind and didn't have any eye."

"How are you on singing?"

"I used to sing in the queer."

"You mean the quire."

"I sang so queer they didn't 'quire me any longer."

"Did you ever go out to Denver Colar and Elbow? That's a great place to go and get cured of consumption. I know a lady that went out there. She only had one lung. She stayed six months and came home with two."

"That's nothing. I know a Dutchman that went out there and he only had one lung. He stayed six months; came home with three."

"How was that?"

"He got married out there and brought his wife back. She had two lungs and he had one. That made three."

"I suppose you have heard of the Rocky Mountains?"

"Yes."

"I painted them."

"I heard Pike's Peak about that."

"I have got a good job now."

"What are you doing?"

"I am draughtsman in a bank."

"What do you have to do?"

"Open and shut the windows."

"My father used to run a bank. I was dealer."

"I have got a good job. I am doing short hand in a livery stable. Am taking down hay for the horses."

"Do you know that all great men are some kind of a bug? You take President Roosevelt. He is a big gold bug. You take Bryan, he is a big silver bug. Hobson, he is a kissing bug. Dewey is a lightning bug, and you are a humbug."

"I suppose you would call yourself a big bed bug."

"I got into trouble the other day.   I got Jimmy Jinks to plead my case."

"Jimmy Jinks ain't old enough to plead a case. He is only sixteen years old."

"I know he is twenty-one."

"I say he is only sixteen, for I was up to his house and looked in the old family Bible and saw written in black ink where he was sixteen, and you can't scratch that out."

"I know he has had the seven-year itch three different times and you can't scratch that out."

I used to know a girl her name was May.   May was a lovely girl.   I took her to the theater one night.   And after the show we went into the restaurant to get something to eat.   May she ordered two birds.   After supper we ordered something to drink, she wanted me to give her a toast.   I said, "I am just as happy as two birds in May."

I took her for a ride in an automobile.   We had only gone about three blocks when we ran into a telegraph pole.   We went up in the air about fifty feet.   We came down so fast we both changed our nationality coming down.   I came down a Russian. She fell across a telegraph wire and came down a pole.   When she fell it didn't hurt her a bit.   She was full of safety pins.

I was down to her house one evening; we were sitting in the parlor.   She called me her little shining lamp.   We said a few words, then she turned me down.   Her father came in; he wanted to put me out.   Her brother wanted to trim me.   Just to show them I was game, I went out smoking. Then they said I was wicked.

Her father came right behind me. I ran up the alley. The old man was right after me. I couldn't see him, but I could feel his foot. I ran until I came to a high board fence. I made up my mind I

HOW WE BOTH CAME DOWN

wouldn't run any further. I would turn around and fight him. I put up my dukes. I was looking for an opening; that is, in the fence. He put his fist in my eye. When he took it away my eye was black. I told him he couldn't do that to the other eye. Well, when I got out of the hospital I was sorry I said it.

It was in St. Louis I started for the depot to catch

a train.   I looked at my watch and saw that I had just time to get there.   I jumped in a cab, told the driver to take me to the depot.   After he had gone for some distance I looked out and saw he was going by.   I hollered and told him to stop.   He stuttered,

THE OLD MAN RAN ME UP THE ALLEY

and before he could say "whoa," he was four blocks by.   When I got back to the depot I was ten minutes late.   My train had gone.   I sat down to wait for the next one.   I saw a Jew rush up to the ticket agent and say, "Gimme a ticket to Springfield." The ticket agent said, "What Springfield? Springfield, Illinois, or Springfield Missouri?"   The Jew said, "Vitch is the sheapest?" An old man sitting alongside of me said, "Are you acquainted here in St. Louis?" I said, "Yes." He said, "Do you know a man living here by the name of Smith?" I said, "No, I never knew anybody by that name." He said he used to know a man down in Georgia, up nigh the Virginia line by the name of Smith. He moved somewhere around here. There was an Englishman sitting close to us. The old man asked him if he lived in St. Louis. He said no, he lived in London. The old man said, "London, London, let's see, what part of Georgia is that in?" An old lady rushed up to the depot master and said, "I want to catch the 10 o'clock train." He said, "You can't catch it. It has just pulled out." She said, "It is too bad. There she goes." The depot master said, the idea of her saying, 'there she goes.'" I said, "She is perfectly right. She should say, 'there she goes.'" He said, "Yes, but that was a mail train."

I was riding on a street car, smoking a strong cigar. A lady sitting alongside of me said, "Will you please put out the cigar?" I put it out. I had on a new shoe that was hurting my foot. I pulled it off and began rubbing my foot. The lady said, "Will you light the cigar?"

I was riding on a street car one time between Minneapolis and St. Paul. The car was crowded. There was a lady standing in front of me with a pair of skates hanging over her shoulder. I offered her my

seat.   She said she didn't care to sit down as she had
been skating all day.

"Do you know, that you look like Barnum's monkey?"

"Look here, sir, I can stand to be called most anything, but when you come to say I look like Barnum's monkey you will have to apologize.   Yes, sir;
you will have to apologize."

"All right, I will apologize."

"When?"

"Just as soon as I see the monkey."

"What do you take me for, a fool?"

"No, I never judge a man by his looks."

"Look here, sir, I want you to quit ridiculing and
making fun of me.   I picked you up out of the gutter and have tried to make a man out of you.   I've
done everything I could to help you along.   I have
even put up with your looks in order to make something out of you.   I have went so far as to give up
my beer and free lunch routes in order to look after
you; and now, after all I have done for you, I understand that you said I wasn't fit to live with the
hogs.   What have you to say for yourself?"

"I didn't say you wasn't fit to live with the hogs.
I didn't say that at all.   I stuck up for you.   I said
you was fit to live with the hogs."

While traveling through the state of Missouri a
few years ago, I stopped at a place where the old soldiers were holding a reunion.   There was a crippled
soldier in the crowd.   He was pretty badly crippled.

AT THE UNION STATION, ST. LOUIS.   HE WAS FROM GEORGIA

Some grape shot had hit him in the face and knocked all of one side of it off.   He had lost one leg and both arms.   He had a hook on one arm and a basket hung on it.   He was passing it around among the soldiers and they were donating very liberally. When anyone would drop anything in the basket he would say, "Thank you, comrade, thank you."   He came to where a fellow was reading a paper.   The fellow just ran his hand in his pocket, pulled out five dollars and dropped it in the basket.   He said, "Thank you, comrade, take out your change."   He said, "Keep it."   He said, "What regiment do you belong to?"   He said, "None."   "Why are you so liberal then?"   He said, "Because you are the first Yankee I ever saw that was trimmed up just to suit me, and when I see one I am willing to pay for it."

Do you know that England outdoes every other country.   She has many things to boast of.

What have you in England that we haven't got in this country?

We have got Lords.

What is that?

They are men that don't work.

We have got lots of them in this country.   We don't call them lords, though.

What do you call them?

Tramps.

We have got policemen in England that stand six feet high in their stocking feet.

That is nothing. We have policemen in this country that stand six feet high and never had a sock on.

In England we have got great trees that grow one hundred feet high. There are deer that run through them with horns ten feet across.

In this country we have got trees that grow three hundred feet high and only two feet apart. There are deers that run through these trees that have horns twenty feet across.

How do they do it?

They wait until spring, then the trees leave.

In England we have parks that are so large that it takes six weeks to go through them.

We have got, right here in Chicago, alleys that the health officers never go through.

Speaking of remarkable things, Montana has Great Falls.

———

I have got an uncle. He is an engineer on a passenger train. He is an awful smart man. He uses great judgment when anything happens and always does the right thing. Not long ago while he was running sixty miles an hour he looked out and saw right ahead of the engine a little girl sitting on the track. He knew he couldn't stop in time to save her, so he took a big rope he had on the engine, tied one end around the smoke stack, threw the other end over a telegraph pole, jerked the train off the track, saved the little girl's life, and killed fifty Swedes.

My uncle had another thrilling experience not long ago. He has got long gray whiskers. While he was running seventy miles an hour he saw a little baby sitting on the track just ahead of the engine. **He** knew **he** couldn't stop in time, so he rushed out on the front end of the engine. He crawled down on the end of the cow catcher; he held on with one hand; then he made a grab for the little baby, and what do you suppose happened? The wind blew through his whiskers.

A THRILLING ADVENTURE

You talk about fast riding. I have had some great experience in that line. I remember one time I was seated in the smoking room of the sleeper when the question was asked how fast are we running. There was a difference in opinions of the speed. **One fellow** said he thought the train was making sixty miles an hour. He said it was the fastest he had ever rode. Another fellow said he had rode a great deal faster. He said that he had a girl living at a little town on the line. He was to pass through there on a certain date and wrote his girl to be at the depot to meet him. He was on the train of that date, but it was a fast train and didn't stop at his girl's town. Just before he got there he went out on the platform, got down on the bottom step so he could kiss his girl as he went by. Just as he did the train whistled. He saw his girl standing on the platform. He swung out and tried to kiss her as he went by. The train was running so fast that instead of kissing his girl he kissed a cow five miles away.

Another fellow spoke up and said that wasn't as fast as he had rode. He said he rode so fast that he couldn't see the towns as he went through. We said, "Was that because you were going so fast?" He said, "No, it was because he was locked up in a box car." I said, "You have told about your fast trains, I will tell you about a long train I rode on. It was so long the engine passed the depot on time. It was running fifty miles an hour; when the caboose went by it was an hour and a half late."

CONUNDRUMS.

Did you ever hear the story about the bed? No, I never did. That's where you he.

When is a horse not a horse? When he is turned into a pasture.

What is a pig doing when he is eating?   He is making a hog of himself.

Why do people in Kansas build their pig pens in the north side of the yard?   To keep the pigs in, of course.

Why does a dentist put his teeth in a show case? So the people can see the teeth.   No, it is so they can pick their teeth.

I know a man that shaves twenty times a day. Who is it?   The barber.

They are laying for you.   Who?   The hens.

I went out in the yard to get something.   Picked it up, looked for it, and couldn't find it; came in the house, put my foot down, picked it up again, looked for it and found it.   What was it?   It was a splinter.

Looks like a cat, walks like a cat, eats like a cat, and it ain't a cat.   What is it?   It's a kitten.

What is a kiss?   Nothing divided by two.

Kiss an old maid once—she screams with delight,
Kiss her twice—she will stay up all night,
Kiss her three times—she hollers for more,
She knows how it is, for she has been there before.

I ain't coming over to your house any more.
Why so?
I was coming over to your house yesterday to

borrow your cook stove, and your bull dog ran me up an apple tree.

My bull dog won't bite.　He is fond of children.

I know he is, for I missed two of mine.

He will eat from your hand.

Yes, and he will eat from your leg, too.

I saw him when he was after you.　He was actually wagging his tail.

Yes, and he was barking at the same time.　I didn't know which end to believe.

Do you remember that horse you sold me?

Yes, and I told you he was a good horse, but he didn't look good.

I hitched him up to the buggy the other day and he ran into everything he came to.　I got out and looked at his eyes and saw he was blind.

Don't you remember, I told you he was a good horse, but he didn't look good?

Do you remember that hen you sold me?　There is something wrong with her.　Every day we find her egg broken on the ground.

That is easily accounted for.　While the other hens are at work that hen gets up on the roost and lays off.

Do you know that your brother is crooked?

How is that?

Me and your brother went in the cattle business. We only had ten dollars apiece.

You couldn't buy many cattle with only ten dollars apiece.

We only bought one cattle.　We divided our business.　The head part was to be mine, the hind part was to be his. I had to feed my part. He milked his part and wouldn't give me any of the milk. I got even with him. I killed my part and his part died. That's why I say he's crooked.

That's a nice suit of clothes you've got on. Where did you get it?

My tailor in New York made it. That's a nice siut you've got on. Where did you get it?

Carrie Nation made it.

Carrie Nation isn't a tailor.

Yes she is, didn't she make all the saloon men close?

My wife used to pick my clothes.

My wife used to pick my pants.

This morning I pumped for a half an hour and couldn't get any water. Can you tell me what was the matter?

The sucker was on the wrong end.

You ought to sleep good, you lie so easy.

How is your father?

He is dead.

How did he die, for want of breath?

He died a lying.

He kept up the same old business.

He knew within thirty minutes of the time of his death.

Who told him, the sheriff? I remember your father and some more men went out west to buy up horses. The other men came back. Your father's a hanging around out there somewhere yet.

My father was a lightning calculator. He could figure up any sum in his head. He didn't have to use a pencil and paper to figure up anything. All he had to do was to scratch his head and he had it.

Didn't they ever get away?

My father was a very peculiar man. He wouldn't eat fish. In fact he couldn't stand the smell of fish. We couldn't have fish in the house where he was at all. One morning he came down stairs and said to mother, "I thought I told you not to cook any more fish." She said, "I am not cooking fish." He said, "I know you are, for I smell fish." She said, "That isn't fish you smell, it's the perch in the bird cage."

Father had been reading a great deal in the papers about Carrie Nation breaking up joints out west. He thought he would go out and help her. He got an ax and started down the street with it on his shoulder. He slipped and fell and broke his leg right next to one of the lowest joints in town. The ax flew off the handle the same time father did. It went up in the air and came down and stuck in the top of his head. He was laying there on the sidewalk. The people all gathered up around him. Some said it was suicide; some said it was an accident; I said it was the first time anything like that had ever entered father's head. My father was a great wrestler. He could throw most anybody down. He threw his whole family down and everybody he owed. The last wrestle he took was with a milk wagon. He grabbed at the wagon and fell in the spring. He went to see a doctor. The doctor told him if he

hadn't of fell in the spring the fall would have killed
·him.

———————

There was a terrible accident down at the railroad
the other day.

What was it?

A fellow was lying on the railroad track; a train
came along and cut all of his left side off.   They
took him to the hospital and he got fixed up.   Now
he is all right.

I was standing in the hotel office the other day
when a man rushed up to the proprietor and said,
"I'll bet you ten dollars the next President is a repub-
lican."   He wouldn't bet.   The fellow rushed up to
the clerk and wanted to bet him that the next President would be a democrat.   He wanted to bet me
that the next President would be a populist.   I
wouldn't bet either.

Did he get taken up?

Yes.

Who by?

The elevator boy.

A friend of mine got part of his hand cut off the
other day.   He has a good job now.   He is doing
shorthand.

Suppose you were out in a boat with your wife
and mother, and the boat should strike a snag and
sink.   Who would you save, your wife or mother?

In that case I would save my mother.

That is right.   The world is full of women.   You
could easily get another wife, but where, oh where,

under the great canopy of heaven, could you ever get another good, kind and loving mother?

Suppose you were out in a boat with your wife and mother-in-law and the boat should strike a snag and sink. Who would you save? Your wife or mother-in-law?

I would save the snag. The world is full of women. You could easily get another wife and mother-in-law, but where, oh, where under the great tin can of New Hampshire, could you get another good, kind and loving snag?

Not very long ago I was out boat riding. There were seventeen people in the boat. The boat capsized. We were all struggling in the water. I took out a bar of soap and washed ashore.

People are getting very strong nowadays. I saw two men go out in a boat and pull up the river.

Are you married?

Yes, I have been married three times. Next July I am going to celebrate the Fourth. My last wife has got black eyes. I give them to her fresh every morning. I see your wife wears bloomers.

She has got a perfect right.

How about her left?

By the way, who were those two young ladies I saw you on the street with?

Oh, did you see me?

I should say I did. You are a sly old fox. By the way, do they paint?

One of them does; the other one gives music lessons.

Did you hear about the big fire?

What was it?

A rubber store burned. My brother was working in it. He was in the tenth story when he discovered it was on fire. My brother has great presence of mind to act on the spur of the moment. He put on a pair of rubber boots and another pair and another pair until he had on twenty pairs. Then he went to the front window and jumped out. When he struck the ground he bounced up as high as the building and came down and bounced up again. He bounced up and down for twenty-four hours. We had to get a gun and shoot the poor fellow to keep him from starving to death.

That's nothing. My brother was working up in the soap factory. He was up in the fifteenth story when he discovered it was on fire. My brother, he has great presence of mind to act quickly on the spur of the moment. Just think of it. My brother up in the fifteenth story of the building with it all on fire. What do you suppose he did?

What did he do?

He just picked up a bar of soap and came down the lather.

I took a trip out west to the Pacific Coast. I went out by the way of that big Mormon town. The one they call Salt Lake City. That is a fine place to live in. You can have just as many girls there as you want to, and they don't get jealous. I would rather be a lamp post in Salt Lake City than to be the Mayor of Oklahoma City. If I had a **ticket** for

Salt Lake City and one for Heaven I think I would go to Salt Lake.

While on my trip I met a young lady on the train. She said she was from down in Knebrasky; said she was going out nigh Seattle. She said her uncle had writ her to come out. I told her that was a

IN SALT LAKE CITY

pretty nice country out here. She said that was what she 'lowed; said she took the bed car one night. She says, "We are running a pretty good hick'ry now, you can't hardly count the trees." About that time the conductor came through and said, "Let down your windows, we are coming to a tunnel." She wanted to know which side it was on?

When we got to the tunnel she said, "What is the rules out in this country? You take it back in Knebrasky when a girl is talking to a boy you had to have a lamp burning or you was talked about." I said, "The rules is out here to blow it out." She said, "You seem to understand the rules tolerably well." I guess she thought I was going to talk love to her. She said she was done already promised to one man back in Knebrasky.

The next morning when I woke up I looked out and said, "We are in Oregon." A fellow said, "How do you know?" I said, "Because it's raining." I looked to see if I had my umbrella with me. I knew if they caught me in Oregon without an umbrella I would be arrested. Speaking about umbrellas, that is something everybody knows how to raise in Oregon.

There was a fellow on the train from Tom Bean County, Texas. He had never been shod, whenever he laughed he would shed Texas stears. He said he came over that route by the way of Pieblo and Pocotolo; said he had to change cars and lie over night at Pieblo; said he didn't like the kind of tavern rules they had in Pieblo. He said the one he stopped at they made him write his name in a big book, and there was some writing in the room that said, "Don't blow out the gas"; said he didn't blow it out and they charged him two dollars for letting it burn.

He said down whar he came from everybody carried a pistol. He said his uncle came out to the west on a emogrunt train in the early days and fit

FROM TEXAS. HE WAS THE LIMIT

HE WOULD OF DONE TO OF RODE ON THE SLOW TRAIN

the Indians at Tacoma.   He said the people at Tacoma wanted his uncle to stay there and settle, he said, after his uncle came back to Texas.   They liked him so well they rit him several letters asking him to come back and settle.   Said his pap had fit all through the war.

I said, "The war is most all forgotten about now."
He said, "No, it wasn't forgotten about for his pap had fit all through it."   He said, "besides his sister Samanthy had picked up with one of them Yankee soldiers and married him and they moved out here to a place called Spooken Falls.   I don't suppose you ever heard of that place before but it's out here somewhere for Sister Samanthy writ a letter and said it was in Washington up near the Canadian line.   He said he would like to know what kind of a place it was.   A gentleman sitting in the next seat told him that Spokane was a good place to go through after night, providing you don't stop over ten minutes.

I used to think that all the funny things happened in Arkansaw.   But after seeing the man from Texas I came to the conclusion that Arkansaw wasn't the only pebble on the beach.   For there is a round rock in Texas.

The way they catch fish in the Columbia River, mostly they club them to death.   Men get two dollars and a half a day for clubbing salmon.   Some places along the river they use what is called fish wheels.   They are big wheels that are turned by the current of the water, but a great deal of the time the wheels refuse to turn on account of the salmon coming so thick that they block the wheels. I thought that was a fish story, but they showed me.

There are many points of interest along that line. I remember some of them. Multnomah Falls for one. They are eight hundred and sixty feet high. The train stopped right opposite the Falls so as to

THE WAY THEY CATCH FISH ON THE COLUMBIA

give all the passengers a chance to see them. While we were stopped there gazing upon that marvelous sight, the conductor was telling us all about them. He said, "Do you all see that log running out from the top of the falls?" We could all see it. He said, "Not very long ago, a young lady walked out on the end of that log; it broke off with her. She fell to the bottom eight hundred and sixty feet below." An old lady said, "I suppose she was mangled?" The conductor said, "No, just a sprained ankle was all." She said, "How was that?" He said, "When she fell her dress just formed a parachute."

MULTNOMAH FALLS, 860 FEET HIGH

When the train started the conductor told the young lady from Knebrasky that she would have to change cars at Portland for Seattle. She said, "Is that on the map?" The conductor got mad and walked away, and wouldn't answer the question.

A gentleman sitting across the way that runs a big brewery at Portland said, "Young lady, what was it you wanted to know?" She said, "The conductor told me that I would have to change cars at Portland to go to Seattle. I would like to know where that is." He said it was right next to his brewery.

> Then she cried I will Seattle,
> As she arose Tacoma hair,
> But her Butte was in Montana,
> Beneath a Tombstone in Arizona.
> Then she cried Walla Walla
> I am going to the St. Louis fair,
> But if I ware my New Jersey,
> What will Delaware.

When the sun shines in Portland they always take a photograph of it. When I was there the latest picture of the sun was nine months old. I asked a fellow in Portland what the people did when it rained so much. He said they just let it rain.

I saw a lady with a cataract on her eye, a ripple in her hair, a creek in her back, a spring in her dress and a notion in her head.

While I was in Portland I met a friend of mine. He invited me out to his house for dinner. He told me he lived at $2\frac{1}{2}$ Mud Street.

I asked him where that was.

He said it was 2.30 Clay after a heavy rain.

It rained so much while I was in Portland that my money was wet. It was due in the morning and missed in the evening. Yes, it does rain a great deal in Portland, but with all the rain it is a beautiful place. The sun is out of sight.

Mount Hood can be seen in the distance reared in all her splendor, with her sky-piercing

peak towering above the clouds capped with ever-
lasting snow, glittering and gleaming in all her
majestic grandeur, captivating and sublime.

While I was in Seattle a man· asked me how I
would like to go to Klondike and dig gold.   I told
him I wouldn't mine.   I thought I would go up there
and take the gold cure, only I was afraid the ice

PORTLAND, OREGON

would make funny cracks at me.   I think all poor
people ought to go to Alaska.   They can cut just
as much ice up there as anybody.   They can walk
around with the seals.   I went up there with a friend
of mine.   He had been there before and located a
claim.   He gave me half interest in it.   We had lots

of money in our mind. I was in the mining business in Alaska. I was mining my own business. Alaska is the coldest place I ever saw. While I was there a man set a bucket of boiling water outside to cool. He left it for two minutes; when he came back the water was froze; the ice was still warm. Whenever a man goes to Alaska and makes any money he has to come down to Seattle and get it thawed out. While I was in Dawson City there was a man froze to death. They decided they would cremate him. They fired up the crematory. When it got red hot they put him in the oven. After he had been in there for several hours they supposed he had been thoroughly cremated. They opened the door. When they did they saw him sitting up in one corner of the oven with his coat on. He said, "Shut that door. This is the first time I have been warm since I have been in Alaska."

Me and my uncle left New York for Seattle. We had three million dollars between us. That is, between us and Seattle. When we got to Seattle we spent the three million the first night. Then we woke up.

Seattle is a great place. It is different from any place I ever saw. It gets so foggy there you can't see attle. You can travel over there for miles and miles without riding on a railroad train, street car or hack. You can go from Seattle to Alaska by sound. Seattle is a very pretty place. They say it is a prettier place than Portland because it is laid out nicer, but you wait till Portland has been dead as long as Seattle and she'll be laid out just as nice. Whenever the people in Seattle want to take a trip to the country and have a nice quiet time, they go to Port Townsend.   That is a good town to sleep in.   It is so quiet, no steam whistles or any thing to bother you.

I went from Seattle to San Francisco by steamer. It is a delightful trip going down.   As I went down everything seemed to be coming up.   When you get your ticket that includes a trip up and down between Seattle and San Francisco; you go up and down on the same trip.   I have always heard you couldn't get full on water, but that is a mistake; you can get just as full on water as you can on land.   The fellow that was in the next cell to me—I mean stateroom.   I was thinking about another trip I took one time.   He must have got terribly full from the way he coughed up.   If I had seen an island within five miles distance I think I would have jumped overboard and took chances of swimming to it.   The second day out a young lady fell overboard.   When she struck the water a big shark came up and looked at her and swam away and never bothered her.   He was a man-eating shark.   After I landed at Frisco I lived on sea-food for three days.   I could see it through the windows.   I got so hungry I could have eaten the cracker off a whip.   The fourth day I was there I stopped at the Palace Hotel.   When the clerk showed me my room I had a notion to eat the jam off the door.   The landlord insulted me the first day. He accused me of eating the soap.   He told me I stole the soap out of the washroom and ate it.   I told him I didn't eat the soap.   He said, "Yes you did, for I can see the lye on your lips."   I went in the café and called for a drink.   The bartender asked me if I had any money.   I told him that was all right.   When I poured out my drink the bartender told me that I could buy whiskey cheaper than the proprietor.

I went down to Frisco just for a little change and a rest. The street-cars got the change and the hotels got the rest.

I took a walk through China-town. I saw a China-man fall down and break his arm just above the opium joint. They picked him up and carried him into the house. When they set him down he fell over against the stove and hit the pipe.

I was walking along Market street without a thing on my mind only my hat. When one of the prominent men of the town spoke to me, he advised me to leave town for my health. He said it wouldn't be healthy for me if I stayed. So I decided I would go and in order to see the scenery to a good advantage I thought I would walk. As San Francisco is almost surrounded by water I had no choice of routes. I naturally went south.

My first stop was San Jose, the garden spot of California, ten girls to every boy. Every day there is either ladies' day or bargain day. Boys, if you are a little slow and can't catch a girl go to San Jose; if you don't catch one there you are certainly a dead one. I took a stroll through the park, I laid down on the grass beneath a beautiful palm to rest, I fell asleep, I had a sweet dream, I dreamt I saw a beautiful maiden coming towards me, I could feel her soft hands upon me, I could feel her winding her golden net around me, I thought she was going to steal me. When I awoke the dog-catcher had me.

When I got to Los Angeles I got insulted. As quick as I stepped out of my special car they filled it with sheep. I stayed there two years one summer; yes, it was all one summer, no winter.   Every day a holiday, one continual round of pleasure. Now, as I have reached the land of sunshine, the ideal spot, I will get a stop-over and take a rest.

In a little cemetery in a far western state lies a brakeman who was killed in a wreck.   Before starting out on his last run he asked for rest, the company being short of men his request could not be granted. It was on a Decoration Day that myself and a few more railroad boys went to the cemetery to place a few flowers on his grave.   When we came to it I saw upon his monument this inscription: "Don't bother me, I have kicked for rest."

This world is but a game of cards,
Which each one must learn to play;
When hearts are trumps we play for love,
No sorrow mars our game.
When diamonds are trumps 'tis then we play for gold;
Great fortunes are won and lost, we are told.
When clubs are trumps look out for war
On both land and sea.
When spades are trumps our little game is played,
For the spade is saved to dig the gambler's grave.

Fare thee well, me lovely Arkansaw,
I bid thee adieu, adieu;
I may emigrate to Hell-ena, Montana,
But I'll never come back to you.

ND - #0040 - 011222 - C0 - 229/152/6 [8] - CB - 9781528463362 - Gloss Lamination